# NOAH'S ARK

By Barbara Shook Hazen
Pictures by Tibor Gergely

**GOLDEN PRESS**
Western Publishing Company, Inc.
Racine, Wisconsin

Long ago, when the world was new, there lived a man named Noah.

Noah was a good man. He spent his days in peace and happiness with his family.

God saw this and was pleased.

God also saw great wickedness in the world, in the other men and women who lived then. He saw selfishness and cruelty.

God said to Noah, "I am going to flood the earth and destroy every living thing on it — except for you and your family and two of each kind of animal.

"It will rain for forty days and forty nights. To save yourselves, you must build an ark. Build it three stories high, with many rooms inside. Make it waterproof with pitch. Stock plenty of food for all those aboard."

Noah heard and agreed to do as God had directed.

He and his family started to work. They hammered and sawed and cut and nailed. Plank by plank they put the boards in place, till an ark began to take shape.

Finally it stood, on dry land, the biggest ark ever made.

When they had finished the ark and waterproofed it, Noah and his sons searched for two of every kind of animal—every beast that walked and every bird that flew.

Noah also gathered enough food for many months — hay for the horses, grain for the cattle and meat for the lions and tigers.

There was even a pile of carrots for the rabbits and plenty of sweet clover for the honey bees.

Then in marched the animals two by two,
The long-necked giraffe and the kangaroo,
The walrus and the wallaby too —
Up the ramp two by two.

Up the ramp flipped two slippery seals,
And after them came two electric eels,
Badger and beaver, bear and gnu —
Up the ramp two by two.

And when all the animals, and Noah, his wife, and his sons, and his sons' wives were safely inside, the door of the ark was shut tight.

It began to rain, a drizzle at first, changing to a steady downpour.

Oh how it rained! It rained in rivers. It rained in sheets that beat against the sides of the ship.

And the wind howled. And the thunder roared. And the lightning flashed in jagged streaks across the sky.

The ark was lifted by the rising water and began to float.

All life on earth was destroyed except for Noah and his family and the animals on the ark.

The storm raged with a fury. White-capped waves tossed and flung the ship — this way, that way, up and down.

The animals grew uneasy. The wolves howled, the horses whinnied and the tiny field mice squeaked with fear.

Even the great striped tigers crouched in a corner and meowed like little kittens.

Only the lions did not roar or cry out. But they, too, were afraid. They didn't move or eat or even twitch their tails.

Oh, the great joy of being free! The horses pranced. The kangaroos leaped. And the penguins flapped their wings. Even the heavy hippos kicked up their heels as they paraded down the ramp onto dry land.

Under the arc of a beautiful rainbow, the animals went their separate ways.

The antelope and mountain goats bounded to the high hills.

The brown bears ambled off to the woods along with the raccoons,

the weasels and the woodchucks.

The crocodiles crawled toward the mud, and the lions and tigers raced to see who would be first to reach the deep, dark, steamy heart of the jungle.

The tame animals, the cattle, horses, sheep and goats, stayed close by Noah because he needed them.

And for a long while, the birds circled overhead, filling the air with song, before they flew off to find new homes.